Edited by Laura Baker

Designed by Ailsa Cullen

Production by Charlene Vaughan

Written by Malachy Doyle

Illustrated by Rowan Martin

This edition published by Parragon Books Ltd in 2014 and distributed by

Parragon Inc.
440 Park Avenue South, 13th Floor
New York, NY 10016
www.parragon.com

ISBN 978-1-4723-5078-7

Printed in China

PEEK -A- BOOK

PaRragon

Bath • New York • Cologne • Melbourne • Delhi
Hong Kong • Shenzhen • Singapore • Amsterdam

Once upon a time,
there was a book about
a sleepy, snoozy cat.

Then a dog from
another book
spied her sleeping ...

... and he started to chase her!

Woof!
Woof!

So the cat jumped right out of her book and into another book.

Far, far away, deep in the woods, there lived three bears, who had gone out for a stroll while their porridge cooled down.

And guess who slipped onto the page and licked the smallest bowl clean? Not Goldilocks … but Cat!

And guess who tore in after her, landed on a chair, and broke it? Dog!

Cat saw Dog, so she sprang
straight into the biggest bowl …

… and into a giant's castle!
"Fee fi fo fum!" yelled the giant.
"I smell a CAT!"

He chased her all around the castle
and down a beanstalk.

But Dog was there at the bottom,
barking his head off.

The startled giant slipped
and came tumbling down. Cat jumped
lightly on top of him, bouncing over
Dog and into …

... a forest!

Racing through the trees, Cat passed a boy tossing crumbs over his shoulder, as he and his sister walked through the woods.

"Hansel," whispered the girl. "I think we're being followed."

And they were! By Dog, who was gobbling up every one of the crumbs.

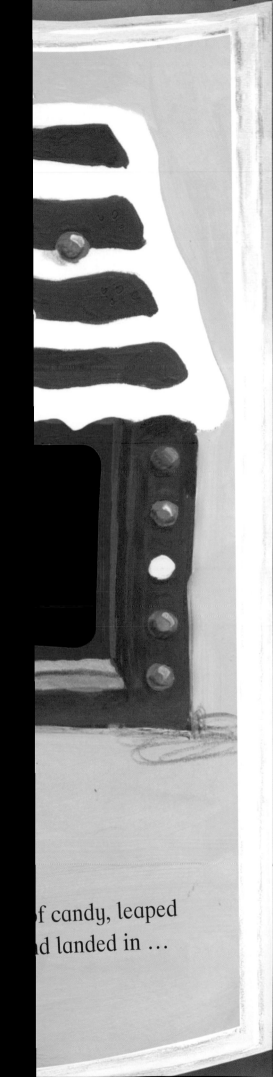

f candy, leaped

d landed in …

She t—

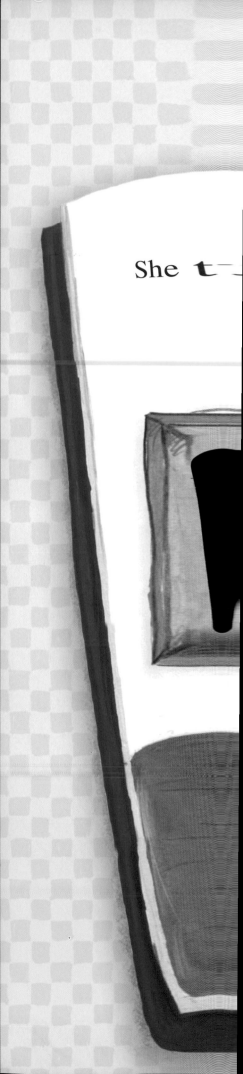

But it wasn't Grandma
who answered.
"All the better to see you
with," said CAT!

She hopped out of bed and ran
right into …

… a little house made of straw!

"Let me in," cried Dog at the door, "or I'll huff, and I'll puff, and I'll blow your house down!"

"Not by the fur on my chinny-chin-chin!" shouted Cat.

So Dog huffed, and he puffed …

Woof!
Woof!

Ah …
choo!

But Cat escaped, just as the straw fell down all around Dog.

Soon Dog followed
Cat to a river.

"Who's that trip-trapping over my bridge?"
grunted a grumpy troll.

"Just me," said Cat.

"Well, I'm going to eat you up!"
roared the troll.

"Oh, don't do that," said Cat. "A big
fat Dog will be here soon, and he'll be
much tastier than me!"

And off she went, over the bridge
and down the path.

But Dog snuck safely by the
troll and continued the chase.

"Run, run, as fast as you can," meowed Cat,
scampering away from Dog, an old man, an
old woman, and a pig. "You can't catch me,
I'm a ginger-red CAT!"

She skipped and she skidded,
straight into …

… a grandfather clock!

Dog started clambering up after her, when …

((Bong!))

The clock struck one, and Dog fell down.

Hickory Dickory Dog!

Cat sprang into a story with
seven dwarfs.

"One, two, three," counted Dog,
trying to find her. "Four, five, six,
seven, EIGHT!"

Cat was feeling a bit tired after all
that running and chasing, but she
managed to jump into one more
book, called …

Cinderella!

She found herself at a ball in a beautiful palace. Dog leaped onto the page and landed right in front of her.

"Let's dance," he said gently.

And guess what? Cat found out that he was actually very nice.

"I was only chasing you because I wanted to play," Dog said, as the clock struck midnight. "All I ever wanted was to be your …"

"... FRIEND!"

And they both lived
happily ever after in
their very own story.

THE END